This Walker book belongs to:

_____

_____

_____

For Nana and Grandad

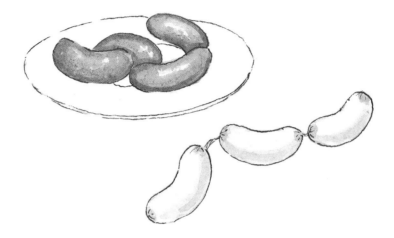

First published 1993 by Walker Books Ltd
87 Vauxhall Walk, London SE11 5HJ

This edition published 2009

2 4 6 8 10 9 7 5 3 1

© 1993 Siobhan Dodds

The right of Siobhan Dodds to be identified as author/illustrator of this work
has been asserted by her in accordance with the Copyright, Designs and Patents Act 1988

This book has been typeset in Garamond

Printed in China

British Library Cataloguing in Publication Data:
a catalogue record for this book is available from the British Library

ISBN 978-1-4063-2332-0

www.walker.co.uk

GRANDAD POT
SIOBHAN DODDS

WALKER BOOKS
AND SUBSIDIARIES
LONDON • BOSTON • SYDNEY • AUCKLAND

ring
ring
ring

"Hello, Grandad Pot. Mummy said I could come to tea and stay the night and if I'm good you might make me a chocolate cake. Chocolate cake is my favourite food. Don't worry, Grandad Pot – I won't be any trouble."

What a surprise for Grandad Pot! Polly is coming to stay.

Chocolate cake

Ingredients
10z chocolate
10z butter
10z flour
10z sugar

Quick, quick, quick!
A chocolate cake for Polly.

ring
ring
ring

"Hello, Grandad Pot.
Can Henry come too?
He won't be any trouble.
Henry has a big plaster
on his knee. He was
doing cartwheels in the garden and he
fell over. He didn't cry. He told me that
jelly and ice-cream will make his knee
better. Don't worry, Grandad Pot.
Henry can sleep in my bed."

What a surprise for
Grandad Pot!
Henry is coming
to stay.

Quick, quick, quick!
Jelly and ice-cream for Henry.
Oh! and a chocolate cake
for Polly.

ring
ring
ring

"Hello, Grandad Pot. Can Rosie come too? She won't be any trouble. Rosie isn't feeling very well today. I think she has a cold. She sneezed four times this morning. She likes banana sandwiches best. Don't worry, Grandad Pot. Rosie can sleep in my bed too."

What a surprise for Grandad Pot! Rosie is coming to stay.

Quick, quick, quick!
Banana sandwiches for Rosie.
Jelly and ice-cream for Henry.
Oh! and a chocolate cake
for Polly.

ring
ring
ring

"Hello, Grandad Pot.
Can George come too?
He won't be any trouble.
George has red spotted
shorts and a big, fat tummy.
His favourite food is sausages.
Don't worry, Grandad Pot.
George can sleep in
my bed too."

What a surprise
for Grandad Pot!
George is
coming
to stay.

Quick, quick, quick!
Sausages for George.
Banana sandwiches for Rosie.
Jelly and ice-cream for Henry.
Oh! and a chocolate cake
for Polly.

Knock
Knock
Knock

"Hello, Grandad Pot.
This is Henry,
this is Rosie,
and this is George."

What a surprise
for Grandad Pot!
Oh! and …

what an enormous tea for Polly!

"Goodnight, Grandad Pot.
It's lots of fun coming to stay."

Other titles by Siobhan Dodds

ISBN 978-1-4063-1677-3

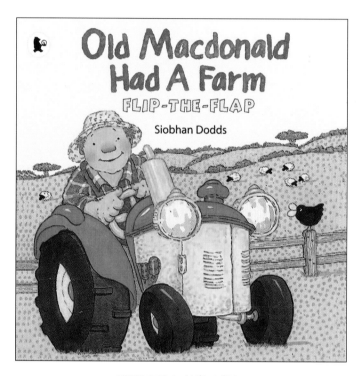

ISBN 978-1-4063-1680-3

Available from all good booksellers

www.walker.co.uk